PIRATES
on the Farm

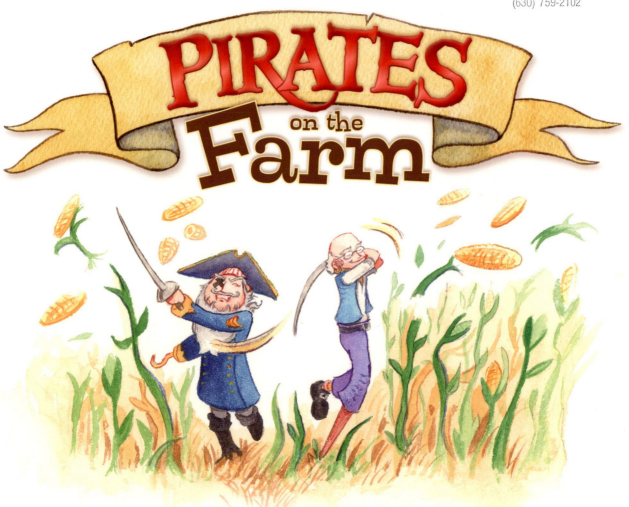

WRITTEN BY **Denette Fretz**   ILLUSTRATED BY **Gene Barretta**

ZONDER**kidz**

ZONDERVAN.com/
AUTHOR**TRACKER**
follow your favorite authors

For Hannah and Jesse

—DF

For my cousin, Gary, who steers his own ship

—GB

ZONDERKIDZ

Pirates on the Farm
Copyright © 2013 by Denette Fretz
Illustrations © 2013 by Gene Barretta

Requests for information should be addressed to:
Zonderkidz, 5300 Patterson Ave SE, *Grand Rapids, Michigan* 49530

ISBN: 978-0-3107-2348-6

Published in association with literary agent Blair Jacobson of D.C. Jacobson & Associates LLC, an Author Management Company. www.dcjacobson.com

Zonderkidz is a trademark of Zondervan.

Editor: Barbara Herndon
Art direction and design: Kris Nelson

Printed in China

13 14 15 16 17 18 /DSC/ 21 20 19 18 17 16 15 14 13 12 11 10 9 8 7 6 5 4 3 2 1

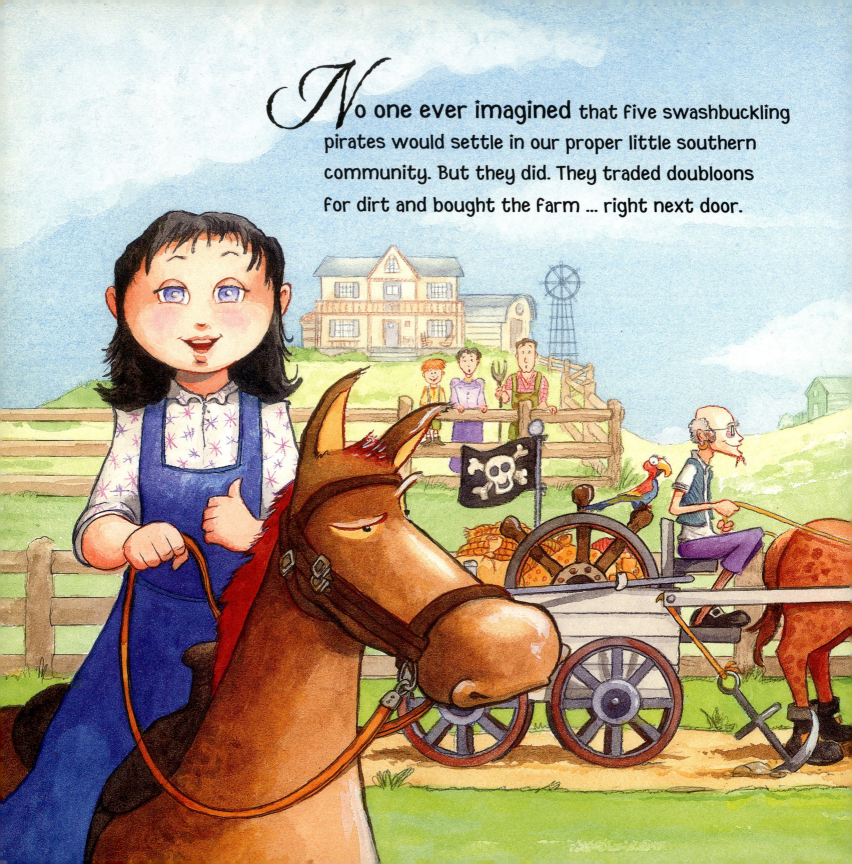

*N*o one ever imagined that five swashbuckling pirates would settle in our proper little southern community. But they did. They traded doubloons for dirt and bought the farm ... right next door.

Joey, my little brother, was delighted. He stopped calling me "Sis" and started calling me "Matey."

Mother was horrified. She rode into town and asked Sheriff Harlow if there were any laws prohibiting pirates from owning land.

There weren't. So she hurried home, took her pine box full of money down from the kitchen cupboard, and hid it under a floorboard.

~~MOVE TO TOWN FUND~~

MOVE AWAY FROM PIRATES FUND

Dad strolled over the hill and helped the pirates unload their trunks.

Within a week, the pirates next door had built a new barn. We'd never seen anything like it. Mother called it "disgraceful."

Joey begged to walk the plank.

Dad nailed down loose boards, patched a hole on the poop deck, and rescued a piglet from the crow's nest chicken coop.

The pirates next door were not clever farmers. They didn't know anything about:

planting seeds

watering

milking a cow

riding a horse

harvesting corn

... or shearing sheep.

Dad, however, was an old-hand at farming. He worked alongside the pirates as often as he could and gave them his *Farmer's Almanac*.

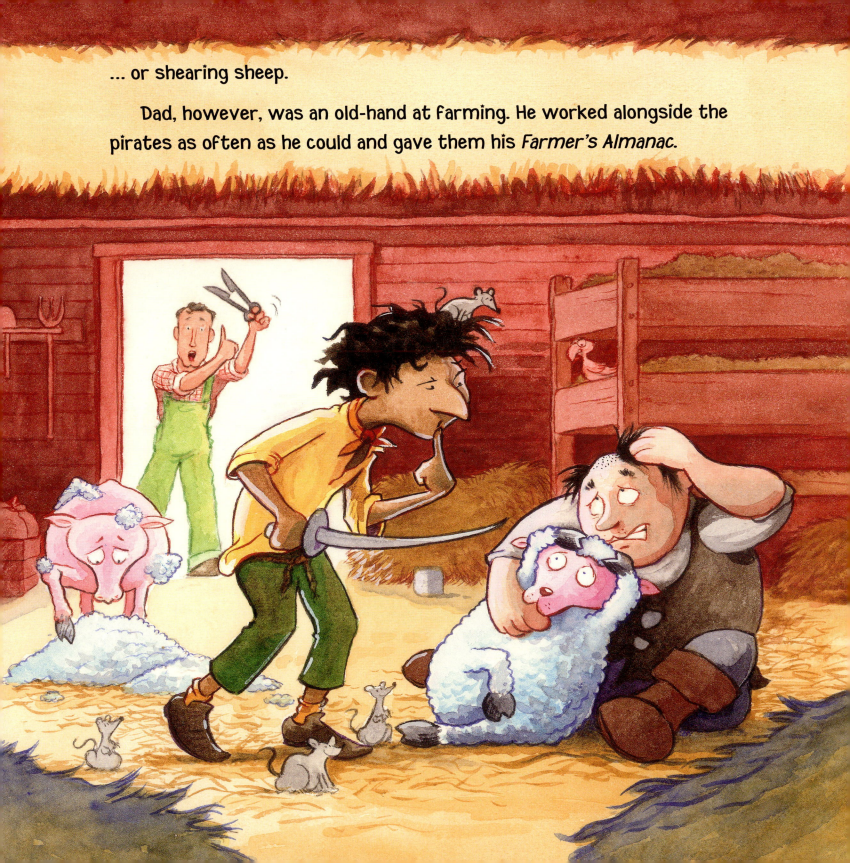

The pirates next door lacked social savvy.

My whole family was shocked the night we discovered the seadog
definition of dinner "invitation."

The grub was ghastly: hardtack, crusty cheese, and fish stew. The pirates beamed as Digger scooped a fish head onto each of our plates.

Mother screamed.

Joey asked if you're supposed to eat the eyeballs.

Dad asked for seconds.

Our church has never been as silent as the Sunday five pirates showed up and plopped themselves down in the front row.

Mother and Mrs. Mayfield began organizing a "Ban the Buccaneers Brigade."

Joey tied on an eye patch.

Dad went forward, shook the pirates' hands, and sat down beside them. He didn't change pews when they belted out "Yo-ho-ho" as the words to every hymn. And he didn't flinch when they looted the offering. He just added money and passed the plate.

When the pirates tried to impress the town's teacher by enrolling in school, the Brigade was alarmed.

And they were aghast after the rogues tried out the merchandise
at Mayfield's General Store.

But the Brigade called an emergency meeting after Riverdale's annual Christmas pageant was commandeered by five pirates who did not understand why anyone would put a baby in a feeding trough.

In the spirit of the holidays, Joey requested the pleasure of the pirates' company for New Year's Day dinner. It was the first time anyone had invited them anywhere. Ever.

Mother protested, but Dad insisted.

The pirates amazed all of us when they arrived with: a parrot for Joey, a one-of-a-kind weather vane for Dad, a scrimshawed whalebone for me, and a beautifully bejeweled hat pin for Mother.

Despite Stretch's tales about seasickness and scurvy, the evening was wonderful—until Sheriff Harlow and the Brigade arrived with a court order demanding the pirates pay for:

stolen offerings,

runaway livestock,

and damages to Mayfield's General Store.

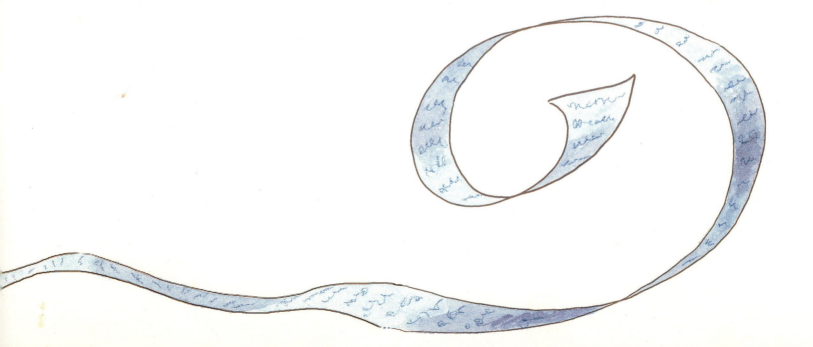

And if they couldn't pay, the Brigade would sell the pirates' farm and set them sailing.

But all the pirates' doubloons had been spent on land and livestock, planks and plows, grain ... and gifts for friends.

Fortunately Mother had an idea ...

Now Mother asks the pirates to supper every Saturday.
She serves delicious salmagundi, bone soup, and hardtack.

Joey shows off Jolly Roger's latest tricks.

Dad and the pirates discuss the weather before playing spirited games of knucklebones.

I practice the art of scrimshaw.

As for the pirates, dinner invitations are much more civilized, and Reverend Springer often finds surprises in the offering plate.

The pirates train horses, shear sheep, and grow gorgeous vegetables ... although Dad still supervises livestock branding.

They are successful farmers.

Joey howls, "Maroon the landlubbers for mutiny!"

Mother shakes her head and marvels, "Who'd of thought?"

But Dad says, "When you plant love, it grows."

I'm just glad we're friends with the people next door.

STRETCH'S TOTALLY TRUE SEADOG DEFINITIONS

Buccaneer . . . . Dis just be a swanky posh name fer pirate.

Commandeer . . . . . To be takin' by force. What Digger will do to yer salmagundi if ye be a pokey slow eater.

Crow's Nest . . . . . . A ship's towering tall perch fer givin' a bird's eye view of mermaids, enemy vessels, or land. I not be recommendin' spittin' off it when Captain Greybeard be walkin' below. Ask Ratty.

Doubloons . . . . Gold pieces, all which be de exclusive restricted property of me own self, Stretch. If ye be discoverin' me lost misplaced coins, ye best be returnin' 'em … or yer nose be riskin' a swift personal visit from Digger's shovel.

Eye Patch . . . . What ye be needin' to wear if Digger's shovel be missin' yer nose. See Doubloons.

Farmer's Almanac . . De landlubbers' treasure map fer growin' bountiful splendiferous crops.

Hardtack . . . . Crackers or biscuits made fer lastin' on lengthy long voyages. Pooch's recipe holds de prestigious esteemed record fer de most teeth chipped in one bite.

Jolly Roger . . . . A pirate ship's smilin' skull and crossbones flag. Poor disgraced Roger aboard The Black Aye be missin' several teeth. All that grinnin' be irritatin' to Digger's nerves.

Knucklebones . . . . . A game like jacks which ye play with ankle bones from sheep. Clever intelligent players be lettin' Digger win.

Landlubber . . . . De Official Legitimate Pirate Dictionary changed this word from "land lover" out of tremendous great respect fer Captain Greybeard—who not be good at pronouncin' his vees.

Maroon . . . . [1] Leavin' a mischievous ornery pirate on a deserted island to enjoy spendin' time with himself. [2] De kindest thing Digger will do to ye if ye touch his shovel. Ask Ratty.

Matey . . . . Friend. Joey be me matey.

Mutiny . . . . Replacin' a ship's captain without his permission. If ye be de polite type and want to be askin' de captain first, see Walk the Plank or Maroon.

Pieces-of-Eight . . . Silver coins. If Captain Greybeard be feelin' stingy mean on payday, he be choppin' de pieces of eight into pieces-of-sixteen or twenty-four.

Poop Deck . . . . De raised upper deck area built above a cabin. Its name be fittin' fer The Black Aye barn ship, as it be situated below de crow's nest chicken coop.

Rogue . . . . Someone who be likin' his own rules better than de king's. Or queen's. Or governor's. Or admiral's. Or sheriff's. Or Brigade's.

Salmagundi . . . . . . When supper be stewed onions, anchovies, boiled eggs, apples, cabbage, and pickled vegetables tossed with oil and vinegar; de crew not be spoilin' their favorite meal by askin' Pooch why his secret ingredients be movin'.

Scrimshaw . . . . De art of drawin' handsome pretty pictures into whalebone. It be healthier fer de artiste if de whale not be usin' de bone at de time. Ask Ratty.

Scurvy . . . . A ghastly horrible disease suggestin' that ye listen to yer dearest darling Mother and eat yer fruits and vegetables.

Seadog . . . . A veteran skilled sailor who be worth his salt. Captain Greybeard be worth his salt, but de crew stopped Digger from sellin' him just in time.

Swashbuckling . . . Flashy, loud, rowdy, and adventurous behaviors flaunted by respectable excellent pirates—which be rulin' out Pooch.

Walk the Plank . . . [1] What happens if ye get caught tryin' to replace de captain without his permission. [2] Captain Greybeard's device fer forcin' Ratty's quarterly bath.

Weather Vane . . . . A rooftop gadget most beneficial fer helpin' ye avoid de direction downwind of Ratty.

Dear Parents,

On several occasions when my children disobeyed God's Word, I wanted to stare them down, rattle their shoulders, and screech, "You should know better!" Thankfully, a sane little voice always countered, "How will they know unless you teach them?"

Deuteronomy 6:6–7 (NLT) enlightens parents that teaching children God's commands isn't a one-time-and-they've-got-it job. "You must commit yourselves wholeheartedly to these commands that I am giving you today. Repeat them again and again to your children. Talk about them when you are at home and when you are on the road, when you are going to bed and when you are getting up." I pray that *Pirates on the Farm* helps you bind the second greatest commandment, "Love your neighbor as yourself," on the heart of your child (Matthew 22:39).

Pirates on the Farm is written as a humorous, thought-provoking parable to engage your child's imagination and allow you to extract the biblical analogies that are spiritually and developmentally appropriate for him. Several ideas for discussion topics are:

- Who is my neighbor? Read and discuss Luke 10:25–27.

- What character most consistently lets his light shine before the pirates? How? (Matthew 5:12)

- How were Mother's actions Christ-like when she paid the pirates' bill? (1 John 3: 4, 5)

- Sometimes the pirates caused trouble for the Sanders family. Do others' actions ever make it hard for you to obey the command to love your neighbor? How?

- List some ways to show love to a "neighbor" this week.

My greatest hope for this story is that it inspires parents and their children to demonstrate God's love to the "pirates" in their lives.

As you diligently plant and water, may God cause your child to grow.

The grace of our Lord Jesus Christ be with you,
—Denette Fretz